LEVEL 1 READER

MOBY SHINOBI

NINJA IN THE KITCHEN

PAPA PEPPY'S Pizza

by Luke Flowers

SCHOLASTIC INC.

TO MI AMORE, TESS.

"When the moon hits your eye, like a big pizza pie . . ."
Thank you for cheering me on through all of life's
mishaps and victories. PLUS you make a delizioso pizza!

Library of Congress Cataloging-in-Publication Data

Names: Flowers, Luke, author, illustrator. Title: Ninja in the kitchen / by Luke Flowers.
Description: New York, NY : Scholastic Inc., 2017. | Series: Scholastic reader. Level 1 |
Series: Moby Shinobi ; [2] | Summary: Told in rhyme, Moby Shinobi tries to put his ninja skills
to work helping Papa Peppy in the pizza shop, but everything he does ends in ruined pizza—
until the key to the cabinet where the secret sauce is stored gets lost. Identifiers: LCCN 2016045583|
ISBN 9780545935364 (hardcover) | ISBN 9780545935340 (pbk.) Subjects: LCSH: Ninja—Juvenile
fiction. | Helping behavior—Juvenile fiction. | Pizza chefs—Juvenile fiction. | Stories in rhyme. | CYAC:
Stories in rhyme. | Ninja—Fiction. | Helpfulness—Fiction. | Pizza—Fiction. | Humorous stories. | LCGFT:
Stories in rhyme. | Humorous fiction. Classification: LCC PZ8.3.F672 Ng 2017 | DDC [E]—dc23 LC
record available at https://lccn.loc.gov/2016045583

10 9 8 7 6 5 4 3 2   17 18 19 20 21

Printed in the U.S.A.   40
First printing 2017
Book design by Steve Ponzo

3

Toss! Hop! Twist! I can kick through brick!

Swish! Slice! Flip! Watch my ninja trick!

Zoom! Leap! Catch! Help is always near!

Papa Peppy, I heard your shout.
My ninja skills can help you out.

8

Moby thinks of his ninja throw.
He grabs the balls of pizza dough.

Moby thinks of a ninja sword!
He leaps up to the cutting board.

Moby thinks of how ninjas fly!
He stacks the pizza pans up high.

ZOOM!

FLIP!

23

In the back, Moby hears a PLINK!
A shiny key fell down the sink!

Do not worry about the key.
You have a super ninja—ME!
PAPA PEPPY'S Pizza

Moby thinks of a super kick.
He knows the perfect ninja trick.